www.FlowerpotPress.com
DJS-1209-0186
ISBN: 978-1-4867-1775-0
Made in China/Fabriqué en Chine

Does your school have a place to go to find new friends to play?
Ours does! It's called the Buddy Bench. It works a special way.
When looking for a friend or two to come and play a game,
Find someone on the Buddy Bench, say hi, and ask their name.
Ask them if they'd like to play. There's a good chance they agree.
The bench is how they tell the world, "Hey, come and play with me!"

I learned about the Buddy Bench one ice-cold winter day.

It was almost time for recess, and I couldn't wait to play!

I looked quickly out the window and could not believe my eyes.

It had snowed and snowed all morning. The storm had been a big surprise.

I live in a town in Texas, where there is never lots of snow.

When I saw it piling up outside, I couldn't wait to go!

I got bundled up real quick—hat and coat on, laces tied.

When I heard the bell for recess, I took off to get outside.

I yelled, "C'mon!" to all my buddies as I sprinted down the hall.

But my friends stayed in the classroom. They don't like the snow at all.

So I headed for the Buddy Bench I'd heard so much about.

A girl named Shae just giggled when she heard me loudly shout:

"Who wants to play snow football or really any other game?

Anything that's fun to play—to me they're all the same."

Shae laughed because she knew something that I did not yet know.

She said, "Some games can be really fun if you embrace the snow.

I used to live where it is cold from Christmas until May.

I LOVE the cold! I LOVE the snow! And I know fun games to play!

Some summer games don't work too well. It helps to think it through.

If you want to play, I'll show the way, and you might learn something new."

Shae said, "Snow baseball's kind of tough. Snowballs explode on wood.
Snow basketballs are tricky, too. They don't bounce like they should.
But I know something that's really fun and will show you how to do it..."

Then I interrupted Shae before she talked me through it.
I screamed out, "YES! That would be a blast!" because somehow I could tell
that when it came to winter games, Shae knew them really well.

Shae told me all about the way they played at her old school.
And the way that she described it made the winter sound so cool.
Up north they'd build a fort from snow to play capture the flag
or use the fort as their home base when playing snowball tag.

Sometimes they'd stomp out snowshoe tracks and use those tracks to race
or build a funny snowman and play stick the carrot on its face.
I laughed as she explained to me the fun things they would do.
Just when I thought I'd heard them all, she mentioned something new.

Shae said, "One day, when it snowed a bunch and we didn't have a sled, somebody had a great idea to use a tray instead!"

I thought a tray sled sounded awesome and I couldn't wait to play!
So we ran and asked the lunchroom helpers to please loan us a tray.

We took the trays, ran up the hill, jumped down on them, and flew!
I laughed so much my belly hurt. It was so much fun to do.

We went up and down and up and down. The trays worked really well.

We would have loved to stay all day, but then we heard the bell.

On our way back in, I KNEW I had a great new friend in Shae.

So tray sledding was actually the SECOND best thing that happened on that day.

I also learned another thing the day of all that snow:
You don't know who the new kids are or know the things they know.
So if you see a Buddy Bench, you should maybe check it out.
Whoever's there might want to play and wants a friend, no doubt!

The Buddy Bench is actually a popular spot at school.
It's an easy way to meet new friends and a really useful tool.
It's not just for the new kids. I sit there once in a while,
just waiting for a brand new friend to greet me with a smile.

The Buddy Bench exists to give kids a place to go where they can meet new friends. It is great for kids who are new to school, kids who are feeling shy or lonely, or kids who are just looking for a new friend to play with. It is a place where they can meet kids who are feeling the same way they are or where they may be invited by other kids to join in a game on the playground. Over the past few years, the Buddy Bench movement has spread worldwide. Buddy Benches continue to pop up at schools and playgrounds all across the United States and Canada and on almost every continent around the globe!

If you know a place that needs a Buddy Bench, get a group together and make it happen! There are lots of organizations that can help.

A Buddy Bench can be any color, shape, size, or material you can imagine! Some Buddy Benches are made from wood, others are made from metal, and there are even some made from recycled plastic bottle caps! Buddy Benches can be painted, named, or even dedicated to someone special! Each Buddy Bench, like each child who sits on it, is unique!

Ways to Use the Buddy Bench

There are no specific rules when it comes to using a Buddy Bench, but there are plenty of strategies kids can use to ensure that they use their Buddy Bench effectively!

IF YOU ARE SITTING ON THE BENCH:

* LOOK AROUND

  Other kids may not see you sitting on the bench, so if you see a friendly face or a fun game, go introduce yourself and play.

* SAY YES

  If someone comes to greet you, you should always be friendly and try to get to know them. They are looking for a friend, too.

* TRY SOMETHING NEW

  Always try a game or activity suggested by your new friend—you might find a new game you love!

* DO A DOUBLE TAKE

  If you see someone sitting on the bench next to you, make a plan to play a game together.

IF YOU SEE SOMEONE SITTING ON THE BENCH:

* KEEP YOUR EYE ON THE BENCH

  As you play, periodically check the bench. If you see someone sitting down, go over and greet them.

* HAVE A PLAN

  Go over to the Buddy Bench with a game or idea in mind to share with your new friend.

* INTRODUCE YOURSELF

  Be sure to share your name with your new friend and ask for theirs in return.

* INVITE YOUR NEW FRIEND TO JOIN YOU

  Share your activity idea or game with your new friend and invite them to join you!

* INTRODUCE THEM TO YOUR OTHER FRIENDS AND TEACH THEM HOW TO PLAY

  Make sure your new friend feels welcome. Introduce them to your friends and teach them how to play the game or complete the activity you suggested.

* MAKE MORE FRIENDS

  Now that you have made one new friend on the Buddy Bench, why not make more? Continue to check the Buddy Bench whenever you can and encourage your friends to check the bench, too!

THE BUDDY BENCH

Does your school have a Buddy Bench? If not, do you think your school should have one? Why or why not?

Have you or someone you know ever sat on a Buddy Bench?

If you don't have a Buddy Bench at your school, can you remember a time you would have liked to have a Buddy Bench?

Have you or someone you know ever made a new friend by meeting someone on a Buddy Bench?

What would you say to someone you saw sitting alone on a Buddy Bench?

What would you want someone to say to you if you were sitting alone on a Buddy Bench?

If you could design your own Buddy Bench, what would it look like?

WHERE FRIENDSHIPS BEGIN

NEW FRIENDSHIPS GROW HERE

THE BUDDY BENCH